PEANUT
the Penguin

For my little peanuts, Mia and Luca,
who inspire me every day, in every way.

First edition published October 2021

Library of Congress Control Number: 2021910121

ISBN: 978-1-954805-06-4 (paperback)
ISBN: 978-1-954805-07-1 (e-book)

Printed in the United States of America
10 9 8 7 6 5 4 3 2 1

Cover and text design by Laurie Entringer

Bold Story Press, Washington, DC 20016
www.boldstorypress.com

PEANUT
the Penguin

Written and Illustrated
by Aruna M. Lepore

BOLD STORY PRESS
Washington, DC

Once there was a little penguin. His name was Peanut.

Peanut lived happily with his mother, father, and sister on a rocky, sandy shore.

There were other penguin families that also lived on the shore.

Peanut loved his family, just as they loved him, and he enjoyed doing everything with them.

Peanut spent each day playing penguin games, swimming in the cool ocean water, and resting on the sunny rocks, just like all the other penguins.

But there was one thing that Peanut liked to do that no other penguin could do.

He liked to sing.

Now, all penguins sing. Some make short, sharp shrieks, while others make long, low howls. But Peanut had an unusual and beautiful singing voice. His songs were sweet melodies of whistles, unlike any ever heard.

When Peanut sang, he thrust his little chest out, held his head up, took a deep breath, and whistled a most magnificent tune. His voice was magical!

But there was one problem. Peanut enjoyed singing at night.

This was a problem because at sunset, when the evening skies turned orange, pink, and purple, all the penguins huddled together with their families to sleep.

But Peanut stayed up to sing! His beautiful melodies floated through the cool night air.

On some nights, Peanut's mother woke up and said to him, softly, "Peanut, we love your singing, but it keeps all the other penguins awake."

So, Peanut stopped.

And on other nights, when Peanut forgot and sang again, his father said, sleepily, "Peanut, your voice is beautiful, but penguins need to sleep now."

So, Peanut stopped.

In the mornings, angry penguins waddled over to Peanut and his family.

"Why does Peanut have to sing every night? He always wakes us up!" they complained.

"I am sorry," said Peanut, softly.

"This has to stop!" grumbled a large penguin one morning to Peanut and his family. "If you don't stop singing at night, we shall have to ask you to leave this shore!"

This made Peanut very sad. He loved to sing, and he loved to sing at night.

"But why at night?" asked his mother, after the angry penguin stomped away.

"Because it's very quiet," explained Peanut, "and it's the only time that I can share my gift of singing."

"I understand," replied his mother. "Your voice is beautiful, my sweet Peanut, and you should be proud of it. But," she continued, "perhaps singing at night when penguins are asleep is not the best time."

Peanut thought about this. His mother was right. Singing at night made him happy, but it made the others angry. And he did not want the angry penguins to make his family leave the shore that was always their home.

So Peanut tried to sing during the day. But the daytime was the noisiest time at the shore! All the penguins on the shore squawked and cackled all day long.

When Peanut tried to sing, he could not even hear himself. He thrust his little chest out, held his head up, took a deep breath, and whistled. But all he could hear was the sound of all the other penguins!

Poor Peanut gave up. He decided not to sing. He awakened penguins if he sang at night, and no penguin could hear his voice during the day.

Peanut's mother noticed that he was sad and very quiet. He did not play or swim as he did before.

His mother hugged him close. "What's wrong, Peanut?"

"I really miss singing," said Peanut as he began to cry.

"Peanut," said his mother, gently, "this evening, at sunset, will you sing softly to your sister, just until she is asleep?"

Peanut was surprised by this. "I thought you didn't want me to sing at night," he sniffled.

She hugged him closer. "I never wanted you to stop singing," she replied, softly.

She wiped his tears and looked at his little face. He began to smile. "I will sing softly to her, Mama. It can be a lullaby."

That evening at sunset, Peanut sang softly as his sister looked at him with sleepy, happy eyes and drifted off to sleep to the sounds of his quiet melody.

When his sister was asleep, Peanut whispered to his mother, "I enjoyed that, Mama."

The next morning, Peanut's mother said, "Thank you, Peanut, for singing your sister to sleep last night. Could you do that every evening?"

Peanut's eyes widened. He had an idea! "Mama! What if I sing a quiet lullaby to all the little penguins? I can stop when they are asleep."

"What a wonderful idea!" clapped Peanut's mother.

And so, that evening, at sunset, when all the little penguins were ready to sleep, Peanut whistled a soft, sweet melody that floated quietly through the air.

All the mothers and fathers looked up from their little family clusters and began to shake their heads when Peanut started to sing again!

But this time, Peanut sang just until the little penguins yawned, and then with sleepy, happy eyes, they drifted off to sleep.

Then Peanut stopped singing, and his mother put her flippers around him, and he, too, snuggled and went to sleep.

The very next morning, some older penguins came waddling over again to Peanut and his family. The oldest and largest one marched up.

"Peanut was singing again last evening," he bellowed. "We would like to speak to him."

Peanut appeared shyly from behind his father. His mother and sister joined him.

"Young penguin," began the old, large penguin. "You sang again last evening."

"I did," said Peanut, ever so quietly. "I'm sorry. I thought it would help the other little penguins fall asleep. I didn't mean to disturb you. I won't do it again. I—"

"Oh, no!" interrupted the old, large penguin. "But you must!"

Peanut looked at him, surprised, a teardrop just falling from his eyes.

The penguin continued. "Your quiet lullaby did help all the little penguins fall asleep. You have made us all very happy!"

Peanut wiped away his tear. "You are not angry?"

"Oh, no, little penguin, not at all," replied the old penguin, "When you sang at sunset, we heard your splendid voice. We hope you will sing your lullabies every evening!"

"I would be happy to!" said Peanut. He looked up at his mother, who smiled at him. His little face was shining with joy.

And so, the little penguin named Peanut gave the penguins all around the shore the gift of his wonderful voice every evening, just at sunset.

He thrust his little chest out, held his head up, took a deep breath, and softly whistled his sweet melodies that floated through the night air.

And when he was finished, he snuggled to sleep with his family, happy to bring the joy of his gift of song to all the penguins that lived on the rocky, sandy shore.

CPSIA information can be obtained
at www.ICGtesting.com
Printed in the USA
LVHW071701070722
722977LV00002B/53